By Author

Charles Wesley Smith Jr.

Preface

This book has been written with the intent to inspire the uninspired and to bring enlightenment to those who are in a dark place.

We often go through life doubting ourselves and convince ourselves that the situations that we are in are acceptable.

The truth is that it takes self-belief and self-motivation to transpire and bring forth what has already been inside of us.

About The Author

Charles W. Smith Jr. is an avid entrepreneur and successful business owner of two local businesses in the city of El Paso, Texas.

The first being "GON" God or Nothing LLC and the other being LMS Studios.

Charles was raised by local Pastor C.W. Smith SR. a Doctoral Elect Carol J. Smith. He has one sister Asia Smith and is happily married to his wife LaKesha Smith (2019).

Charles is active within his community and continually participates in local events. The latest being the "El Paso Fashion Week" (2019).

Chapter I

Preparation

Preparation! Sometimes in life we are often too hard on ourselves. We are thrown into a society that continually judges. We are classically conditioned to judge even when we don't want to.

As a young kid I grew up feeling insecure about my smile. Not that I wasn't cute, or handsome, but the fact that my teeth weren't as straight as I would have wished them to be.

Although, it seems to be a minor issue to some, for me, it was the world I lived in and it wasn't a good one.

I found myself being thrown into speaking events at an early age and I felt as if they were forced upon me.

At the time I felt that the system was designed for me to fail, finding myself being embarrassed by having to speak knowing onlookers would look directly at my teeth.

Battling through this insecurity is what the true preparation of what has now become my life.

While attending elementary school, when picture day would come up I recall those moments being full of joy.

I remember being the first one to smile, full of excitement and eager to please my parents.

One particular day I woke up on picture day, only to realize that something wasn't right. My mother noticed that my cheek was swollen and very abnormal.

My loving mother took me to the emergency room immediately to get checked out. Upon arriving at the emergency room, the doctors told me I had to see a dentist immediately.

So there we go, out of the ER on our way to the first available dentist that was open. Once we got there and were seen by the dentist I was told that I had a hole in one of my baby teeth.

It was then my world came crashing down. I wasn't prepared for what would transpire next. Emergency surgery and the removal of my tooth would lead to a mouth full of insecurities.

The dentist said if that one particular tooth stayed in, it would have killed me. I found out that the tooth was severely infected. I was completely devastated.

Although I needed more work done, we were in no position to pay out of pocket nearly four thousand dollars.

From that point on, having missing teeth in the front, it caused me to start speaking differently. I would talk in a way to where my lip would cover the rest of my teeth.

Having to speak in class was very difficult, especially when we would have to stand in the front of the class and present work or answer questions on the board.

I had to come to grips with reality and face the fact that my teeth would remain this way for a very long time.

However, being able to stand in front of people started to give me a little more confidence as a personal trait that I still hold onto.

As time passed, I started to transition from middle school to high school. I had to teach myself to have thick skin.

Preparing for high school wasn't as hard as I thought it was going to be. I felt I had enough confidence within me to change the perspective of others' opinions about me.

I was determined to not to let this minor insecurity deter me for the next four years of my life.

At this point, I was truly blessed to have a cousin who showed compassion for my insecurities about my teeth, and he stepped in to help.

Thank God for family. Although, I found myself trekking across the border to get dental work done, it was actually a relief to know that work was finally getting done to correct my teeth.

If I could recall the amount of surgeries I had on my teeth, I would have to say roughly 6 in total. The first trip in Mexico was a hard one. I was told I would have to get 4 teeth removed so the others could come down like they should've.

After the first surgery, I found myself more heartbroken then before. I thought to myself if this were a good idea. I was wondering why they would be removing teeth instead of implanting new ones.

This process was a hard one to deal with, going back time after time, and surgery after surgery to get teeth removed. I wasn't sure if my mouth was able to handle all of this.

The moment I started to have a sense of joy from this process was when I was told I was going to get braces. The excitement that filled my heart was great.

Once I had the braces on I felt like things were starting to fall into place. As things were going smoother my confidence and self-assurance began to grow again.

I felt like I was able to fit in and even smile more, because at this time braces were almost the norm.

Once I came to the realization that my flaws were acceptable, I began to understand that I wasn't the only one dealing with personal issues and insecurities.

I began to see things in a different light. I started talking a lot more and became more socially engaged. I felt like things were going in a positive direction.

When it came to being in front of people that insecurity that once held me down started to subside; all it took was accepting my flaws.

I began to pick up other hobbies, and capture great moments with close friends and teammates. I felt as if I weren't the odd man out at this point.

Chapter II

Evolution

Evolution! Getting older and getting wiser was happening. I wasn't sure how it was happening so fast but, it was and I had to roll with it. Braces on, shining bright, smiling from ear to ear, I started to evolve from little Charles to Charlay.

Once I started to explore sports, hobbies and other interest, I came to realize that I fell in love with rapping.

No, I didn't want to rap because it was the thing to do at that time, I wanted to rap to move people and inspire people to live out their dreams.

During my high school years I really didn't want to be known as the class clown or the one who got clowned. I decided to evolve.

It was after football practice freshman year, I went to one of the star player's home. Once I was there, I was asked did I want to get in the booth.

The first song that we did was titled "Fat Girls." It wasn't to be demeaning to any particular person, but it turned out to be a major hit around campus and everyone thought my verse was the best.

Once I received feedback from this song, I had to develop a stage name. I knew I wanted it to be close to my personal name without compromising the integrity that I've developed.

Charlay was born. I felt inspired and transformed into a new person behind this newfound persona. My first song as Charlay was *"All About My Business."*

The reason I chose to name this song *"All About My Business."* was because it sparked a fire inside of me that fueled me to release the negative feelings that had manifested inside of me due to my insecurities.

This song was actually a process that helped me evolve into a person that would never get down or discouraged again.

Feeling accomplished and knowing that I was actually good at rapping, I was asked to do an event. I was tasked with performing a 16-minute event.

It was at this point I felt like this was my calling. I also felt as if I were Thee Man. There were girls who never gave me the time of day until I became popular.

It was during my first event, that I encountered my first hardship. During the last song that I was performing I got cut off, and told to exit the stage.

I couldn't grasp why I was asked to exit. Once off stage I asked one of the teachers what I did wrong, I was told that I kept using the N word too much.

At the time I thought since I didn't use profanity that the N word would be an acceptable supplement, it turns out that I was dead wrong.

One of the teachers pulled me to the side and said "Charles, you're very talented, but you cannot use the N word around the school."

I had to go back to the drawing board and revamp my lyrics to be a lot cleaner, but still powerful enough to move a crowd.

From this point, I started the song "Won't Stop," the reason for this song was fueled by anger and a bit of disappointment.

I felt the joy of performing and seeing the crowd's reaction really inspired me to keep on going.

There were over a thousand people that I got to perform in front of, and the negativity from my first performance moved me to keep going and write cleaner raps.

The lyrics to the song are as follows:

Shining I stay brighter

On air like the cypher

All about my team man

All about my priors

Stunting my swag on point

Because I be flyer

Giving credit when it's due

When life's tough

Then I get my pliers

My team we're going higher

Success is my desire

I feel it coming in close

And patients

I don't mind her

From this point going forward and the songs there after led me to perform the homecoming parade and national events. I was even fortunate enough to have my song played on El Paso's Power 102 radio station.

This song became an instant fan favorite. It was used as the theme song for our Friday night-lights football games. This song would really get the team amped up and ready to play.

Wanting to play off of the success from this, I was selected for bigger and better things. I was set to create a song for GenTx. To me this was a big deal; I had the opportunity to start doing videos.

The first successful video I created was a parody to *Bruno Mars: If I was your man*. I was able to display my creativity and show how diverse that I really was.

This also gave me more insight regarding the comfort ability of being seen and heard by viewers all over the world. I felt as if nothing could stop me.

Some would say that I might have even been a bit over confident. However, this parody that was done reached a national level, and received a second place vote among 1500 other students.

I made it my prerogative to make music my number one priority. Having been so close to winning a grant was a bitter sweet.

Going into my senior year of high school, I was able to purchase my own recording equipment. I was beginning to master the art of production as well as videography.

After collaborating with the art director, we came up with the idea creating a video for my senior class so that everyone would have a piece of Charlay to take with them going forward.

The song was titled *"We on one."* We as a body of students faced adversity our senior year. Not only did the city count the football team out, but the city also counted the graduating class out and held us to a lower standard.

This fueled me to snap back in a way that the student body would feel like we stood our ground.

The lyrics to this song are as follows:

Been talked about

Been lied on

Been laughed at

Till my pride gone

Yeah the haters talk

We gon listen

Matador pride

And we ain't finished

Stepped up our game

Having no limits

Made playoffs

Yeah we on a mission

With the heart of a bull

Swagger of a beast

Education to the full

Taks test rest in peace

Chapter III

Determination

Determination! Having graduated high school, I knew that music may not get me to where I wanted to be, however would always be a major part of me.

I knew that I wanted to do something with business. I felt that the influences around me would inspire me to become successful in some capacity.

At this time I became an entrepreneur, I found myself booking events with local churches and even got selected to perform at The Fountains for their grand opening.

These opportunities enabled me to network with prominent people. I was building a strong reputation with great minds and business minded people.

Although, I was progressing, I stayed humbled and committed to my roots. I became the youth director of my home church and motivated the children active in my life.

I would get them involved by doing youth concerts, plays within the ministry. I learned that I didn't have to do anything alone. The youth around me wanted to be a part of the movement that I had going on.

I felt like a true inspiration. These feelings held me to a higher standard. I knew that I had others around me that would look up to me, so in that I made sure that I wouldn't let them down.

As I continued to grow, I was fully aware that I had to carry myself in a respectful manner. Being the son of a pastor I knew that all eyes would be on me.

At this point, I strongly felt that I was on the right track. I started venturing and was tasked to do speaking engagements.

While I was doing events, I found myself starting to get turned down for some of them. I questioned why things were starting to slow down for me.

Then the idea of starting GON LLC came into fruition. I was on my way to work one day two acronyms came into mind; the first being GOA that was abbreviated for God Over Anything, and the latter being God Or Nothing.

I felt moved with GON. When this hit me I called into my job and told them I would be late. I immediately went to my graphic designer to get his opinion on the two.

We both felt that GON would not only be the more marketable solution, but it was the stronger of the two meanings.

Having selected GON we started working on the design and the logo trying to put things into perspective. Once we had the right concept, that's when the birth of GON started.

Starting to transition from Charlay the musician into Charles W. Smith Jr the businessman was a beautiful journey.

I started the process to build a clothing line. The ideology of the clothes that I designed would be to effect the Christian population, and inspire them to have a no shame in representing their lord and savior through their attire.

I started off by ordering fifty shirts; half were in white with the black logo and the other in black with the white logo.

I put together my first event and still felt slightly reluctant and uncertain about if this was the right business move to partake in.

The event I put together was thriving; there were local artist performing, food and tons of entertainment.

Having the feelings of uncertainty lingering, I actually walked away from GON for roughly six months. Although, the event was beautiful I just simply wasn't sure if this was it for me.

One day my mother came into my room and looked at one of the GON shirts hanging up on the wall, and told me that I had to get the ball rolling.

She informed me that there was a local pastor that was interested in using my product for one of his events.

Thank you mother!

I knew that this would open up more doors if it were too successful, in which it was.

I knew that I had to strategically market myself in a unique way and I had to start formulating a plan to build my brand. The next step I took was building a website.

I searched and found a web designer and poured over two thousand dollars into building my website.

A costly hit, but it was worth it. I knew that if people were to take me seriously, they would want to look me up and be able to purchase merchandise online.

While formulating a mission statement, I had an epiphany. I wanted the mission statement to be so powerful that readers would feel moved within their spirit.

The mission statement is as follows:

The purpose of GON LLC is to bring curiosity to the nonbelievers and a wakeup call the believers.

Once I had a strong enough mission statement, I was able to move forward with the remaining processes of running and constructing a formidable business.

The frame of mind I had at this time was to bring awareness to Christ through fashion, music and inspiration. I wanted to let people know that no matter where they were in life that it was always God or Nothing.

I felt moved by reading the scriptures of the bible verses Joshua 24 and 15.

"And if it seems evil unto you to serve the lord, choose you this day whom you will serve; whether the god's which your father served that were on the other side of the flood, or the god's of the Amorites, in whose land ye dwell: but as for me and my house, we will serve the lord." KJV

Powerful; this truly meant a lot to me at the time and still does today. I felt that this verse would solidify what GON is all about.

Chapter IV

Growth

Growth! With growth come growing pains. Starting my new business I went in blind. Not knowing where to start or how to start was a bit overwhelming. Being young and fresh into the business world, I would find myself being lost and getting taken advantage of.

Each step for me was one accomplishment at a time. I felt as if though it was a long and drawn out process, but one that would be very rewarding in the end.

There were days I found myself getting frustrated and wanting to walk away, but the beauty beyond the scars is what kept me motivated.

Taking the necessary steps to get legitimately registered in what seemed like every area was costly. As time went on I started focusing on the motto "Becoming the lion within."

I felt like there was a lot that I had to prove to people including myself.

I found myself developing what would turn out to be a strong brand. I was able to book successful events at local churches and other business events.

One thing I am grateful for was having a mentor, who was able to guide me in the right direction. I was able to learn a bit about networking and relationship building.

I went from selling clothes from a minimal price to a higher end while providing better quality. As my birthday soon approached I was able to put one of the biggest events together.

I single handedly collaborated with other local artist, entrepreneurs, musicians, models and teens within the community, to inspire, motivate and cultivate those around me.

From selling clothes out of the trunk of my car, to being able to host one of the largest events of such in the city to date, I felt accomplished.

Learning different marketing strategies and ins and outs of the business world, I found useful tools like marketing videos, flyers and business cards.

I was able to successfully get an interview on the local news channel ABC KVIA 7. This for me was an extremely proud moment. The specific event title was GON for the city.

When the event started I wasn't sure what the turn out would look like, but to my surprise there were over one hundred and fifty people in attendance.

The purpose of this fashion show was constructed to show people of all backgrounds that you are able to accomplish whatever you put your mind into doing. It may not always be black and white; however, it can be done if you are persistent in the belief of self.

With the success of the fashion show, it opened more doors professionally. A lot of people that missed the event reached out to me in a bittersweet manner.

I was told that the feedback the audience was putting out was of extreme positivity.

Once hearing the positive reviews, it brought me to tears. I felt like for the first time in my life I found what my calling was.

After the fashion show, I felt rejuvenated by the amount of opportunities that was presented. I continually wanted to elevate myself to reach this type of success continually.

As I continued to work my full time real estate job, I was encountering issues that didn't seem fair at the time. In real estate I found that it is a dog eats dog mentality.

I found myself having issues with the broker of the organization that I worked for. I felt as if I were so far down the food chain that I was irrelevant.

I was undermined, belittled and made to feel like my opinions did not matter. I know that working this job I gave it my all. However, I also knew that since I was at the lower end of the business spectrum that I would be made to feel inferior.

Having just fallen short by seven questions short of the real estate license exam, I felt lost. I felt as if I were going to work by force. My heart simply wasn't in it anymore.

During this particular time I felt like life hit me hard. I had gotten in my first car accident. I remember leaving church, taking a few of the members home, and was t-boned.

My body went into shock, and my mind went into a spiral affect. I was a bit furious and relieved that I was able to recover healthily.

My first thought was to thank the lord. My first act was to call my father. Thankfully he came and was able to assist me through this process.

Regarding work, it was a huge disappointment. My jobs first reaction was to cut my hours short due to the lack of transportation I had.

I felt like everything I had worked towards was starting to come undone. I realized that life could be unfair. But, we as people have to keep pushing through.

I knew that the hustler inside of me would prevail and shine bright. I bounced back even better than before; new job, new car and a new mentality going forward.

I became the lion within.

Chapter V

In the mind of a King

King! A song I wrote titled: *"Life of a King."*

Everyday above ground

Is a blessing

Thank you for the losses

And the lessons

Thank you for the pain

That kept me pressing

Team no sleep

Never had time for resting

Success in my blood

Running strong

Through my pores

Lion in my heart

Can you hear the music roar

God give a knock

We distracted by the noise

Word is key

So what you think

Null and void

Praises most high

Keeps the lion inside

Faith when I speak

Keeps me absent from my pride

Boss when I walk

With God on my side

Spitting gospel truth

But your soul living lie

Lord I pray

Pray every day

Your will be done

Keep my mind from astray

My heart be right

And my game be tight

May your word stay true

Keep me focused on the light

Praying on the daily

And for my family

Peace of mind

For better understanding

To be more like you

And to grow in you

Chosen by the best

And subtracted by the few

In you I grew

In you I shine

Lion of Judah

Who gave sight to the blind

Food to the poor

And deaf a peace of mind

This world needs you

We can see it through the signs

Chorus

I be bossed up

Everywhere that I go

I'm a praying man

Let every one of them know

I will not stop

I will continue to grow

GON with no limits

I keep giving them more

I wrote this song two years ago. At the time I wrote it, I wanted to let people know that whatever situations they may be going through are designed to be bigger than them. However within us must rely a bigger God

I also wanted to let them know that in God's eyes we are all kings and queens and it is time for us to take our stand as such.

No matter what the world's depiction or interpretation about us, it is about the Lion that is within us.

A lot of times we often seek validation from others, but I feel as if we should choose to take a closer look within our hearts. We as people should speak positivity into ourselves daily and choose to speak life into our existence.

We need to keep God at the epicenter of our lives; because, he is the cornerstone of our very existence. No matter how old or young or religion we should choose to put God first.

Life is too short to not forgive and carry the burden that hardens our hearts. With God on our side we can accomplish what we set forth.

There is no room for excuses; the frame of mind that I have developed through life's experiences

are; to "Making things happen." We can't wait
around and expect handouts from others.

I leave you with Blessings, Love and Hope.

As always,

Become the Lion Within!

"There are two types of people who will tell you that you cannot make a difference in this world: those who are afraid to try and those who are afraid you will succeed."

-- Ray Goforth

This page intentionally left blank

Forged In The Mind Of A King

First Printing: February 2020

Circle of Trails' Publishing LLC

ISBN: 9798615378515

Made in the USA
Columbia, SC
24 February 2024